4000 Miles

by Amy Herzog

SAMUEL FRENCH

FOUNDED 1830

SAMUELFRENCH.COM

MUSIC USE NOTE

Licensees are solely responsible for obtaining formal written permission from copyright owners to use copyrighted music in the performance of this play and are strongly cautioned to do so. If no such permission is obtained by the licensee, then the licensee must use only original music that the licensee owns and controls. Licensees are solely responsible and liable for all music clearances and shall indemnify the copyright owners of the play and their licensing agent, Samuel French, Inc., against any costs, expenses, losses and liabilities arising from the use of music by licensees.

IMPORTANT BILLING AND CREDIT
REQUIREMENTS

All producers of *4000 MILES* must give credit to the Author of the Play in all programs distributed in connection with performances of the Play, and in all instances in which the title of the Play appears for the purposes of advertising, publicizing or otherwise exploiting the Play and/or a production. The name of the Author *must* appear on a separate line on which no other name appears, immediately following the title and *must* appear in size of type not less than fifty percent of the size of the title type.

In addition the following credit *must* be given in all programs and publicity information distributed in association with this piece:

4000 Miles **was originally produced by
Lincoln Center Theater in 2011,
New York City**

4000 MILES **was written in the SoHo Rep Writer/Director Lab**

4000 MILES first opened at The Duke Theater in New York City on June 20, 2011, presented by Lincoln Center Theatre/LCT3, as a Steinberg New Works Program production, under the direction of André Bishop and Bernard Gersten, and Paige Evans, LCT3 Artistic Director. The sets were designed by Lauren Helpern, costumes designed by Kaye Voyce, lighting designed by Japhy Weideman, sound designed by Ryan Rumery, stage management by Kasey Ostopchuck, general management by Adam Siegel, and production management by Jeff Hamlin. The director was Daniel Aukin. The cast was as follows:

LEO JOSEPH-CONNELL	Gabriel Ebert
VERA JOSEPH	Mary Louise Wilson
BEC	Zoë Winters
AMANDA	Greta Lee

4000 MILES moved to the Mitzi E. Newhouse Theater in New York City, opening on April 2, 2012, presented by Lincoln Center Theatre, under the direction of André Bishop and Bernard Gersten. The sets were designed by Lauren Helpern, costumes designed by Kaye Voyce, lighting designed by Japhy Weideman, sound designed by Ryan Rumery, and stage management by Kasey Ostopchuck. The director was Daniel Aukin. The cast was as follows:

LEO JOSEPH-CONNELL	Gabriel Ebert
VERA JOSEPH	Mary Louise Wilson
BEC	Zoë Winters
AMANDA	Greta Lee

CHARACTERS

LEO JOSEPH-CONNELL – Twenty-one
VERA JOSEPH – Ninety-one
BEC – Twenty-one
AMANDA – Nineteen, Chinese-American

SETTING

September of a recent year – maybe 2007. A spacious rent-controlled apartment in Greenwich Village that hasn't been redecorated since approximately 1968. The key decorative element is books.

AUTHOR'S NOTES

A slash (/) indicates overlapping dialogue. Where the slash appears, the next line begins.

ACKNOWLEDGMENTS

Thank you to the SoHo Rep Writer/Director Lab and especially Pirronne Yousefzadeh; Paige Evans, André Bishop, Bernard Gersten and the wonderful staff of Lincoln Center; John Buzzetti; all the endlessly patient and good-humored Josephs, especially the Midwest branch; my beloved cast; the brilliant Daniel Aukin and his cracker-jack design team; as always, my partner, Sam Gold.

For Pavel and Leepee
In memory of Jay

Scene One

(The middle of the night.)

*(**LEO**, 21, lanky, fit, and dirty, stands just inside the apartment, his laden bike next to him. He is smiling broadly. **VERA**, 91, tiny and frail but not without fortitude, is in her nightgown. Her eyes have not adjusted to the light. She covers her mouth because she hasn't put her teeth in. Her speech is altered for the same reason. She is quite disoriented.)*

(A pause in which he grins and she is uncomprehending.)

LEO. You haven't changed the name. On the buzzer.

VERA. What?

LEO. The buzzer! It still says Joe Joseph!

VERA. So?

LEO. So you should change it. Put your name on there.

VERA. That is my name.

LEO. Your name isn't *Joe* Joseph.

VERA. ...well...

LEO. Just seems like it's time.

(pause)

I can help you with that, if you want. I'm pretty handy.

VERA. *(slurred)* You need a place to stay, is that it?

LEO. Sorry, what?

VERA. *(still covering her mouth, still slurred)* You need a place to stay?

LEO. I can't understand you when you –

(He reaches to move her hand away from her mouth; startled, she draws back, almost losing her balance.)

Sorry.

9

VERA. Will you – wait here.

(She exits, still covering her mouth. He leans the bike against a bookcase and takes off one of the panniers – this takes some effort – it is extremely heavy. He puts it down on the floor noisily. VERA reenters, less disoriented, with teeth, and putting her hearing aid in.)

Are you high?

LEO. What? No.

VERA. Well, it's three o'clock in the morning so I'm just asking. Have you eaten anything in a while?

LEO. I'm cool.

VERA. That's not what I asked you. You've lost weight.

LEO. It's been a long road, but a good one.

VERA. You biked all the way here?

LEO. Pretty much.

VERA. From Minnesota?

LEO. Actually we started in Seattle.

(brief pause)

VERA. There are some mountains in the middle, aren't there, whichever way you go?

LEO. There are. There are.

VERA. I'll get you a banana.

LEO. A – no! Whoa, jet fuel.

VERA. What?

LEO. NO SUCH THING AS A LOCAL BANANA!

VERA. You don't have to yell, it's only when you speak very low or very fast that I can't hear you.

LEO. I'm just concerned about you, I was leaning on that buzzer for quite a while.

VERA. Yes, well, I was asleep, and I didn't have my, whadaya-callit, hearing aid in, and I wasn't expecting you.

LEO. Would you hear a fire alarm?

VERA. What?

LEO. WOULD YOU HEAR / A –

VERA. I heard you, listen, it's – it's the way you're acting I
don't understand, actually, not your...the whole family's been very worried, I guess you know that. Your
mother and father –

LEO. I'm sorry people worried, I am, but that's not something I can take responsibility for?

VERA. You should have called. You should have called your
mother. She's been...she's really been...

(He picks up his pannier, goes to reattach it.)

LEO. *(warmly, apparently sincerely)* Grandma Vera. It was awesome to see you.

VERA. What? – You're –

LEO. It's cool, I don't think either of us has to feel bad about
the fact that the timing isn't right for me to be here.

VERA. You're going to – where will you go?

LEO. I have a tent and a camping stove and a love for the
outdoors, I'll be all right.

VERA. You're in Manhattan!

LEO. Maybe you can give me a tip, somewhere out of the
way?

VERA. There's no place like that! Listen, you're being – put
that back down. Put it down.

(He hesitates.)

You can leave tomorrow, I won't stop you. Just – sleep
here for a few hours, and take a shower, and eat some
breakfast. I can wash those – you smell terrible and I
wouldn't be surprised if you had lice.

LEO. I don't have lice.

VERA. And you don't seem all right to me, you don't...
seem all right.

LEO. *(still smiling)* It's just, if this is gonna be about calling
Jane, and a last minute, hellaciously overpriced plane
flight for which she has to take a valium because she's
a phobic freak, and I wake up in the morning and
she's here with a valium hangover –

VERA. I'm not a reporter.

LEO. Meaning?

VERA. Meaning I'm not a news reporter and I won't call your mother if that's what you're asking me.
But the way you're talking about her, it's really not fair, a lot of people don't like flying.

LEO. Jane and I are at a juncture where more talking is not better than less talking. If that's not something you can understand, I'm saying it's probably best I go set up camp somewhere else.

VERA. I don't agree with it, but I understand.

(pause)

I know what she feels like is…if you're not talking to her, she just hopes you're talking to / someone.

LEO. Oh, that is bullshit, and you know her, and you know that is passive aggressive *bullshit*! *She* wants to talk about it! *She!* I am fine!

VERA. *(with genuine feeling)* Well. I did want to say how sorry I am. That must have been –

LEO. Thank you.

(Silence. This has gotten to him, and she sees it.)

VERA. You what, came over the GW?

LEO. The – ?

VERA. The George Washington Bridge?

LEO. I guess, yeah.

VERA. Was it pretty? At night?

LEO. …Yeah, actually. Yeah. I'm not much of a city guy, but. It was all right.

VERA. I'm – I must say I'm surprised, and this is not a complaint, that you came here, instead of your – I've lost track whether she's your girlfriend or not, the chubby one, isn't she up at / whaddayacallit –

LEO. She's not chubby.

VERA. She's – well she's not *thin.*

LEO. She's healthy, she's / strong.

VERA. I don't see what that has to do with it.

LEO. She's not *chubby*.

VERA. All *right*. I thought if you ended up in New York you might have gone there.

LEO. I stopped by.

(*brief pause*)

VERA. She had another fella with her, is that / it?

LEO. No, Vera, she didn't have – it's just not good timing. It turns out. Which I respect. She said she needed to do some *thinking*. Thinking is good.

VERA. Well it's been a lousy coupla months for you then, between one thing and another.

(*pause*)

Would you take a shower before you get in bed?

Leo?

LEO. What? Yeah. Shower sounds great.

VERA. You all right?

LEO. Yeah! Yeah.

(*He picks up the pack and begins to head offstage. She stops him.*)

VERA. Where are you going?

LEO. Guest room.

VERA. No, that one's my room now.

LEO. I thought that – I thought that was yours.

VERA. Not since Joe was sick. We moved in there for the, whaddayacallit, single beds and I stayed. Has it been that long since you've been here?

LEO. I was here for the funeral. I guess I forgot.

VERA. That was a long time ago.

(*He hesitates.*)

You need anything else?

LEO. No, I –

Grandma –

VERA. Yes?

(His uncertainty dissolves into a big smile.)

LEO. …good night.

(He exits.)

Scene Two

(The next day, late morning.)

*(***VERA*** *enters through the front door with a laundry cart.
She has some trouble maneuvering it through the door
and into the apartment. She is taking care to be quiet.
Once she has gotten the cart in and closed the door, she
goes offstage to* ***LEO****'s bedroom. A pause. She comes back,
satisfied that he is still asleep.)*

*(She takes the laundry from the cart, piece by piece, and
folds it. Bike jerseys and shorts. Those wicking pieces of
athletic clothing. Tiny cycling socks. She regards them all
with some suspicion.)*

*(The phone rings. At the first ring, she tenses, listens
to see if she heard right. At the second ring, she looks
anxiously toward the bedroom where* ***LEO*** *is sleeping and
moves as quickly as she can to the old rotary phone.)*

VERA. Hello.

Hold on.

(She takes her whining hearing aid out.)

Hello.

(mild irritation verging on imperiousness)

Yes, darling, what?

I'm not done with it.

I'm not done with it yet.

I know what time it is, but as a matter of fact my grandson is here so I've been busy.

Yes, well, it was a surprise, he came and surprised me, so.

Well that's – listen –

Hello?

(She looks at the phone.)

Hello?

(She shakes her head and hangs up.)

Pain in the ass.

(She goes back to the laundry and continues to fold, still periodically shaking her head. After a few moments, **LEO** *enters, disheveled but clean.)*

LEO. Hey.

(She continues to fold.)

Vera.

(She looks up with the startled look of half-deaf people who aren't sure whether they heard something, and want to cover if they did, and sees **LEO.***)*

VERA. Oh!

(She fumbles in her pockets for her hearing aid and puts it back in.)

The phone woke you?

LEO. No.

VERA. It was Ginny across the hall. I give her the arts section when I'm done with it and I'm late today. Never mind she's never given me a nickel for it, that's what I get for being nice. She says she's just checking in to see if I'm all right but you know she's really sitting there, stewing, resenting me, she's…well, no good deed goes unpunished, right? Did you sleep all right?

LEO. Mm-hm.

VERA. And then she just hung up! I told her you were here and she said, "Oh I'm terribly sorry" in this – like she was interrupting a big meeting or something and she just hung up without even saying – why it gets to me so much I don't know. She's just…

(She looks for the word, doesn't find it.)

She's really a character.

LEO. Huh.

VERA. But we have an arrangement where she calls me one night and I call her the next, and that way if one of us turns up our toes it won't take until we start smelling to figure it out. Which isn't really a problem for me, because I have the family, but she doesn't have anyone, so I guess I have guilt feelings about that is what it is. And we have a lot in common in terms of the political – we both, in terms of Cuba, and the pro-peace whaddayacallit, and being progressives, we see eye to eye, but in everything else she just drives me nuts.

LEO. You're giving her too much power.

VERA. What?

LEO. That power. You gotta take it back.

(She considers this.)

VERA. Well.

If you stay longer, and I'm not saying you will, I'll show you how to, whaddayacallit. Disconnect the phone in that room, because I do get a lot of calls sometimes.

You look better. *(off his look)* What?

LEO. Good morning, Vera.

VERA. Actually it's after twe –

(He interrupts her with a big bear hug. Surprised, she gives in to the totally unexpected physical affection. The embrace goes on for a little while. She closes her eyes and tries to remember it. They separate. She smiles widely at him)

You smell better, too. What did you think of that bed?

LEO. It was great, great bed.

VERA. That's what I think! You know your uncle Ben and Mel, they want me to get a new mattress. Which they do not offer to pay for. Every time they stay here they complain, and complain.

LEO. I slept like a rock.

VERA. I may quote you on that. I'll end up doing it, though, anyway, or else they'll have an excuse not to visit. You drink coffee?

LEO. Yeah, I'd love some.

(She exits. He surveys the neat little piles she's made of his stuff. He stoops and picks up a box of condoms that's seen wear and tear in his bag. He had forgotten he brought it. She reenters with coffee and a plate with a few breakfast pastries on it, maybe a couple hard boiled eggs.)

VERA. I was glad to see you carry those and surprised they weren't opened. I thought you probably take it black.

LEO. I do.

VERA. Me too, that's how I like it.

(He bites into a pastry.)

Tell me if that's completely thawed.

(He gives her the thumbs up.)

I got a few of those free a month or two ago at the Senior Center, some event, they had a buffet table and at the end they were going to throw it all away, which I did not approve of. It was lucky I thought to freeze them because otherwise I would have had to go out and get you something and I wasn't feeling completely up to it. Some days I'm myself, and some days my head really isn't right, and my balance. It's really disgusting.

LEO. Have you had it checked out?

VERA. What? Oh sure, they're all useless, they just tell me I'm old and I knew that already.

I knew you were sleeping well because you didn't wake up when I brought your whadayacallit out of your room. Moaning and groaning – that thing must weigh a hundred pounds!

LEO. Nah. About twenty.

VERA. Is that all?

LEO. Well that's one of four bags. Total weight's about fifty.

VERA. Fifty *pounds?*

LEO. More when I have food and water.

VERA. And you keep all that on your *bicycle?*

LEO. Yup.

(She can't quite believe this but has no alternative.)

VERA. Doesn't that make it a lot harder?

(He laughs, for the first time.)

LEO. Yeah, yup, that's a yes.

VERA. And you camped at night, is that it?

LEO. Usually. Sometimes I'd meet someone and be invited to crash.

VERA. You ever meet anyone really peculiar?

LEO. What do you mean?

VERA. I don't know, like some crackpot who wanted something weird from you, in exchange for...a place to stay or whatever.

LEO. Like...?

VERA. Like a – whaddayacallit, something sexual, or –

LEO. *What?*

VERA. I would think on the road like that, by yourself, you'd meet all kinds of people.

LEO. I did meet all kinds of people. None of them required sexual favors from me, no.

VERA. If you were a woman it would probably have been different; you probably would have run into all kinds of things like that.

LEO. I know a lot of women who travel alone, Bec has done a lot of traveling / alone –

VERA. Rebecca – well, all right, if you're built like *that*, but I mean a smaller / woman.

LEO. I find if you approach people with love and trust you can count on getting the same things back from them.

(*brief pause*)

VERA. What is that, Confucius, or...?

LEO. It's Leo Joseph-Connell. It's me.

VERA. I'm teasing you.

LEO. Okay.

VERA. I guess it's a sensitive subject.

LEO. Nope.

VERA. Well.

(*pause*)

LEO. You know anything about a climbing wall?

VERA. A what?

LEO. A climbing gym!

VERA. What's a climbing gym?

LEO. It's a – a gym. Where you climb. They have these walls / with –

VERA. Oh, with the funny, and you're in one of those whadayacallit –

LEO. Harnesses.

VERA. Right, I've seen that. Where have I seen that? I saw that and I thought what the hell is that for?

(She gets the yellow pages.)

You want to go today, is that it?

LEO. I was thinking about it. Get the old upper body back to work.

(Now with the yellow pages, she asks this studiously casually, without looking at him.)

VERA. So you think you might stay a little longer, is that it? Would it be under…what would it be under?

(He takes the yellow pages from her, gently, and looks.)

LEO. Yellow pages. Man.

VERA. What?

LEO. Do you have a computer?

VERA. No, I – well yes, I have one, Ben and Mel got it for me, but I'm not, whaddayacallit. They were very happy with themselves for getting it for me but they didn't really show me what to do with it.

LEO. Mac or PC?

VERA. What?

LEO. We'll look at it later.

VERA. You know a lot about computers?

LEO. I don't like them. But I can use them.

VERA. I thought everyone your age liked them.

LEO. Micah never sent an email. His whole life. Which was stubborn as shit, but you have to admire it.

VERA. Did he use the telephone?

LEO. Yeah, but he didn't have a cell phone. I don't have one either.

VERA. I know you don't, I've been hearing about that a lot lately.

(brief pause)

I guess what they say is all this, whatsit, technology is good for…from the standpoint of the people, or the – that you can get the propaganda to the people, the Marxist – I can't find the words, but in terms of Africa, and South America, and places where – that from the standpoint of being progressive and so on and so forth it can be a good thing.

(brief pause)

You know, there are a lot of bad things about getting old, but the worst one is not being able to find my words. I just hate not being able to find my words, I feel like an idiot half the time.

LEO. That it's democratizing.

VERA. What?

LEO. That with the internet, information is free to everyone, it um…de-commodifies knowledge. Which is power.

(He returns to his yellow page search.)

VERA. When you put it that way I think I should learn how to use the computer.

LEO. Marx is cool.

VERA. You think so?

LEO. He's all right.

VERA. Well I think so too.

LEO. When I did that semester at Evergreen I took a class on Marx. Best class I took.

VERA. What did your mother think of that?

LEO. About me studying Marx?

VERA. Yeah.

LEO. Uh, I think she was like, "How is that going to be useful to you, in the future?"

VERA. Oh, dear.

LEO. And I was like, first of all, who knows, and second, I think it's important to understand where I come from, which is where you come from, too, so I'm surprised you aren't more supportive.

VERA. *(delighted)* You said that?

LEO. I did.

VERA. And what did she say?

LEO. You know, as long as I was in college, she was happy, so I think she just shut up.

VERA. She and I don't talk about politics anymore. I always end up telling her how disappointing she was to her father, I don't mean to, somehow or other I just wind up saying it, and I only mean in terms of the political – not *generally*, but then she starts crying and going on about how she always votes democrat, as if that's...it's better we just don't talk about it.

LEO. I find that to be true about a lot of subjects with Jane.

VERA. Well, between you and me. I guess I do too.

(A small moment of enjoying each other.)

But she was always my favorite because she was the littlest, you know she was only two when Joe and I started carrying on together. And she's been very devoted to me, so.

LEO. Is 23rd street pretty near here?

VERA. Matter of fact you can walk there. I guess I should get you Joe's keys.

LEO. Um –

(She doesn't hear him and exits. He prepares himself to ask for something. She reenters with keys.)

VERA. I better show you which one does what, and you'll get it wrong the first few times anyway but you'll eventually learn.

LEO. Okay – I was wondering if you could spot me a few bucks? For climbing?

VERA. Oh. You're out of money, is that it?

LEO. At the moment the flow is low.

VERA. How much do you need?

LEO. I don't know what prices are like around here…I have to rent all the stuff, so like, fifty?

VERA. Fifty *dollars*?

LEO. That's what it would be in Seattle, so I guess…maybe a little more?

VERA. More than *fifty* dollars? To climb up a wall?

LEO. I'm expecting an influx in a couple days so I could pay / you back.

VERA. A what?

LEO. An influx! Of cash, into my account!

VERA. From where?
From your mother? She's still giving you money?
Well…

LEO. Forget it.

VERA. No, / listen –

LEO. Forget it! It's no big deal!

VERA. I'm going to show you where I keep the money, and then when you need some you can just take it and leave a note, all right? So I know how much you took and I won't worry about it.
All right?

LEO. All right.

VERA. And then maybe you can do some shopping, and get the things around the house you like to have for breakfast and so on and so forth.

LEO. Vera, I want to be really clear that I can't stay more than a couple days.

VERA. I understand.

LEO. It's great to rest up, but I need to make it back to Washington before it gets too cold, so.

VERA. You mean, on the bike?

LEO. Yup.

VERA. You're going to go all the way back west on that bike?

LEO. That's the plan.

(*an uncomprehending pause*)

VERA. Maybe if you called Rebecca today, she – since it was the middle of the night, she may not / have –

LEO. It's not / about –

VERA. Seeing as you came all this way to be with her –

LEO. I didn't.

I didn't come all this way to be with her.

VERA. Well I know it wasn't to be with *me*.

LEO. It was to finish something I started. Micah and I started something. I finished it. That's it. People want to make it really complicated but it's not.

(*He gives her a big smile.*)

VERA. If you stayed more than a couple days I wouldn't know what to say to your mother. I don't know what to say to her as it is. So we're in agreement.

I keep the money in Joe's study.

(*She tries to stand, doesn't quite make it up, winds up and stands again. She makes her way out slowly.* **LEO** *stays seated. He is fending off a wave of nausea or vertigo.*)

VERA. (*offstage*) You comin' or what?

Scene Three

(A few days later.)

*(***LEO*** *is lying down, eating something and reading a book.)*

(The sound of a key in the lock. It takes a long time for ***VERA*** *to get the door open. She enters slowly, more off-balance than usual. She is wearing dark clothing. She sees* ***LEO***, *who waves and goes back to reading.)*

VERA. Did you lock the top lock?

LEO. No.

VERA. Are you sure?

LEO. Yup.

(She turns and looks at the door, perplexed.)

VERA. Well, I think you must have and then forgotten.

LEO. I haven't touched the door today, Vera.

VERA. Maybe you did it without really thinking about it.

LEO. Uh, okay, sure, I for no reason / and without thinking –

VERA. You have to speak louder if you want me to hear you.

LEO. I didn't lock the top lock!

VERA. Well…

(flustered)

all right.

LEO. Does it really matter?

VERA. I made sure I didn't lock it when I left, because it's getting harder for me to hold the, whadayacallit, the – *key*, because my hand shakes, which is disgusting, but then it was locked anyway so either you did it or I'm going crazy, which I must admit is very possible.

(She exits toward the bedroom, upset. He sits up. He thinks of going after her, then lies back down and continues reading. She reenters.)

I don't mind if you break something, accidents happen, but nothing drives me crazier than when somebody breaks something and doesn't tell me.

(She exits again.)

LEO. What did I break? Vera?

(He puts the book down and begins to follow her but she reenters on her way to the kitchen.)

What did I break?

VERA. Never mind, just tell me next time, all right?

LEO. Dude, I have no idea what you're talking about.

VERA. Now you're really making me mad.

LEO. Tell me what I did!

(She looks at him with disbelief.)

VERA. The faucet! In your bathroom?

(He thinks hard.)

LEO. The faucet...

VERA. Oh, gimme a break!

LEO. You gotta help me out here, Grandma.

VERA. The whaddayacallit, the...

LEO. The whaddayacallit.

VERA. Don't make fun of me!

LEO. I'm not!

VERA. The...handle, that you turn. It's completely off.

LEO. I thought it was always like that.

(She shoots him an accusing look.)

I did!

VERA. No, it wasn't "always like that." I went in there to clean this morning while you were still asleep because it was filthy, because you obviously haven't cleaned since you've been here, and that was the first time I ever saw it like that.

LEO. It came right off in my hand, I swear I thought –

VERA. Well, just tell me, is all I'm asking, I don't think that's an unreasonable request, do you?

(She exits into the kitchen. Pause.)

LEO. *(He calls off.)* Sorry!

(Loud noises come from the kitchen. LEO decides not to take this on. He lies back down and keeps reading. After a few moments she reenters, still in a state.)

VERA. In case you're interested, I just came from a funeral, so that's where I've been all morning.

LEO. Okay.

VERA. It was for the last of the octogenarians.

LEO. The what?

VERA. There were seven of us, octogenarians, and we had dinner once a month for a lot of years and we were all lefties and there were a lot of memories and laughs and the last one just died, besides me.

LEO. Sorry.

VERA. Yeah, he was a rat, very aggressive, he used to make passes at me with his wife sitting right there. She had Alzheimer's so she didn't mind, but I did. Even so, he was the last one and I don't feel very happy about it.

LEO. You want a hug from a hippie?

VERA. No, I'm all right.

(She goes back into the kitchen. A moment later she reenters. LEO goes to her and hugs her.)

And I spoke to your mother this morning, too. And I did not tell her you're here, even though you were all she talked about, and she's really, whadayacallit, in distress, and I'm not feeling terribly proud of myself.

(He separates.)

LEO. You can't take all that on. You have to let her find her own way.

VERA. Well see, that's not how I think about things. Because I believe in a…a society where…here I go with my words. The point is you help people, it's about the community, it's not about I do what's best for me and you do what's best for you, because…you know the one thing I wasn't thinking when Joe was dying was I better pay attention to what he says, about politics, because I always relied on him to, to make the arguments, and explain the…

(She shakes her head, lost, disgusted with herself.)

LEO. *(gently)* I've been reading this book he edited, about Cuba?

VERA. Oh, yeah?

LEO. It's really interesting. I didn't know this stuff, about their healthcare system –

VERA. Oh, their healthcare is wonderful. And literacy, too.

LEO. Grandpa's introduction is really...I don't remember him that well? You know? But I remember his voice, he had / that –

VERA. Yes.

LEO. Yeah, so I've been imagining his voice reading this, and it's like...so sure?

VERA. Indeed.

LEO. The way he writes, it's...it almost reads as a little hokey, now, because it's so – but I think it must have been cool, to be so, um. Uncynical. Like I think I'm really uncynical, and Micah was definitely totally uncynical, but *you* guys. That's like a whole other level of...I'm definitely learning about Grandpa. It's definitely cool.

(pause)

VERA. Your mother told me something very upsetting about you this morning that I have been debating bringing up with you at all. Do you want to know what it is?

LEO. Not really.

VERA. She said in the beginning of the summer, when you were home for a little while in St. / Paul –

LEO. Oh my *god*, she's / still –

VERA. That you tried to kiss your sister.

LEO. I cannot *believe* she is still fixated on that!

VERA. Well, that was pretty disturbing for Lily, I would think.

LEO. It was – we were all – it was so *not* disturbing, she was not disturbed, and *tried* is not really the – I mean, we

kissed, lots of people were kissing, it was like a sponta-
neous kissing convention, and we kissed, and it was so
not a big deal except for in our totally taboo / laden –

VERA. Well, she's in therapy about it now is all I'm saying.

LEO. I cannot – ! Okay. Okay. Fine. She's in therapy,
because we were both fucked on peyote and we kissed,
once, with totally minimal tongue, and *not* because our
parents are obsessed with the fact that they *don't treat
her differently* just because she's adopted and never
fail to mention that to her for a single day in her life.
Obviously it was the totally harmless and even I would
say pleasant smooch that sent her reeling into identity
confusion. I mean, it's not like I fucked / her.

VERA. She's your sister!

LEO. Yeah! And she's awesome! And I wish she would get
the fuck out of that house!

VERA. You need to learn how to take some responsibility,
you know that? You're right, I've seen the way they are
about the – the fact is, they didn't think they would be
able to have you, when they adopted her, and – there's
a guilt there, and a nervousness, but – you're a sensitive young man and you should be able to understand
that and not be so angry about it. And you should be
able to understand that she's vulnerable, she always
has been, and kissing her wasn't the best idea. That's
all. That's all.

LEO. It's just…it's hard to think of something more em-
blematic of our society, that a kiss expressing real
mutual love between two people is considered destruc-
tive.

VERA. You know better than that.

LEO. I don't, Grandma, and I don't want to.

(pause)

VERA. Rebecca found out about it, is that it? And that's why
she's so mad?

LEO. Bec knows about it, because she was there, and she *also* kissed Lily, incidentally, which was really beautiful, and no, she is not mad, because she's way more open-minded than that.

VERA. And I'm old and closed-minded, is that it?

LEO. You're old, but you could choose not to be closed-minded.

(He goes back to his book.)

VERA. You didn't say anything about the buzzer.

LEO. The what?

VERA. I had the super change the name on the buzzer, since you didn't seem to be getting around to it. It has my name now. Only took me ten years, but it has my name now.

LEO. Uh…congratulations? Sorry, is that – what am I supposed to say?

(Pause. He goes back to his book.)

VERA. Well.

(She stands slowly to go. She exits into the kitchen.)

Scene Four

(Lights up on BEC. *She is not chubby. She is in fact strong and beautiful and hale, though she is also somewhat strung out. She may wear a puffy vest over a sweater. She may wear hiking boots. She may have a Nalgene bottle.)*

(She stands uncomfortably for a long time. VERA *enters, walking slowly with a cup of tea. She sees* BEC *is still standing.)*

VERA. Take a load off.

*(*BEC *sits.* VERA *very gingerly, shakily, places the tea in front of her. She thinks of something.)*

You take sugar?

BEC. *(She does.)* Oh – no –

*(*VERA *sees through this and frowningly exits for sugar.* BEC *drops her head in her hands. Silence.* VERA *returns, slowly, with a sugar bowl and a few packets of sweet and low.)*

VERA. My neighbor across the hall is a diabetic, so I keep this stuff around. In case you watch that sort of thing.

BEC. Thank you.

*(*BEC *helps herself to two heaping spoonfuls of sugar while* VERA *watches disapprovingly.)*

You don't have to – if you have something else you need to do –

VERA. You want me to leave you alone, is that it?

BEC. No, just, I don't want you to feel you have to, like –

VERA. What?

BEC. I don't want to be in your way!

VERA. Well, you're not. Particularly.

*(*VERA *sits as well. They don't know what to say to each other.)*

So you're having second thoughts, is that it?

BEC. What?

No, I…no.

(another silence)

VERA. When I was first married. Not to Joe, to my first husband, Arthur. It was a week or two we had been married and a woman showed up at our apartment with luggage. Arthur said to me, "Oh I forgot to tell you, before we were married I promised I would take her away for the weekend and I didn't want to fink on a promise."

*(**BEC** horrified, **VERA** laughing.)*

So I said "all right," and they went away, and I left my key on the piano and went home to my parents.

BEC. And you divorced him?

VERA. Oh no. He came to my parents at the end of the weekend begging and pleading and I thought it was funny that he had been so stupid so I went home with him.

It wasn't the last time he cheated.

BEC. Of course not!

VERA. When we had been married six months he went out to Hollywood with a woman…oh god, what was her name. She was rich, and neurotic. *Muriel.* He and Muriel went out there to write a screenplay and her father bankrolled them and Arthur never sent me a penny. And I guess they were having an affair because when he tried to end it she threatened to kill herself, and that was a terrible mess. One time we were all at Café Society…

I guess they were back from California…?

And she followed me into a cab and said, "Can't we be friends? It eats away at me that you're angry at me," and so forth. And I said "Listen, Muriel, there are people you like and people you don't, and I don't like you, and I want you out of this cab." And she cried and carried on, this woman who had been sleeping with my husband for two years…

(Long pause. BEC *drinks her tea.)*

Then there was the waitress he met in Arkansas.
And he came home and confessed he was in love
with her, and I said "Listen, she's a hick, you have
nothing in common, I'm sure the sex is terrific
and whatnot but why don't you go back there and
spend a few weeks with her and see if there's really
enough there for you to leave our marriage." And
he did. And sure enough he came back and said,
"You're right, we ran out of things to talk about."
And that was that.

He was a cheater and a drunk, but I liked him till the
day he died.

BEC. *(blurting it out)* I'm not sure what you're trying to tell
me.

VERA. What?

BEC. I don't know what you want me to – why are you telling me this?

VERA. I was just making conversation. I wasn't getting much
help from you.

BEC. But you're going on and on about these – like, par-
ables of tolerance and forgiveness – you should have
left him!

VERA. I did, eventually.

BEC. But you put up with like – and you tell these stories
like you're proud of them.

VERA. *(seeing that* BEC *is truly upset)* Okay, listen –

BEC. This woman, who you tried to push out of a cab, you
should have pushed *him* out of a cab, she was coming
to you / for understanding –

VERA. I see I've struck a / nerve.

BEC. I'm not going to forgive him!

VERA. All right. All right.

*(*BEC *struggling to get control,* VERA *totally unsure what
to do.)*

BEC. I'm sorry, I've been really…

And I can't believe he's fucking late, I can't *believe*…

VERA. Listen, I wasn't trying to say forgive him or don't forgive him. I don't know what you should do, that's your affair.

I was trying to say…men sometimes do things that can be very…but you have to remember that it's more out of stupidity than anything else. It's not, whaddayacallit. Malicious. It's just stupid and childish.

BEC. I guess, um…

(searching for the inoffensive way to stay this)

I don't make those kinds of allowances, based on gender? I wouldn't want anyone to make those kinds of allowances for me, so…

VERA. I suppose you think I'm very backward.

BEC. No –

(The sound of a key in the lock. BEC hears it immediately and prepares herself, VERA looks around suspiciously to see what she heard. LEO enters, his pants covered in dirt. Both women look at him. He grins.)

LEO. I found a community garden.

(VERA winds up and stands.)

VERA. Excuse me.

(She exits into her bedroom slowly. LEO heads in for a kiss, BEC dodges him.)

BEC. I told you I have class at two.

LEO. Am I late?

BEC. I can't miss any more class.

LEO. I said I'd come up to you.

BEC. And I said I didn't want you in my apartment.

(He grins.)

LEO. I brought you something.

(He produces a small, sad, dirty pumpkin from his hoodie pocket. He approaches her very slowly and extends it to her. She takes it.)

BEC. What do you want me to do with this, Leo?

LEO. Love it. Nurture it. Teach it what you know.

Make a pie.

(She throws it back at him. He catches it. It is unclear whether some of the tension is broken or if she is angrier than ever.)

I miss you all the time. I think of you in *college*. I think about whether they have left-handed desks for you.

BEC. They do.

LEO. That's good.

BEC. Sometimes right-handed people sit at the left-handed desks and I get really pissed.

LEO. Bastards.

BEC. Yeah. I'm like, you're not just hurting me, you're hurting yourself.

(They smile. This is their thing.)

LEO. You like it?

BEC. I don't want to talk about college with you, Leo.

LEO. Why not?

BEC. Because you're just gonna be, like, disdainful.

LEO. I'm not!

I wanna hear.

BEC. It's...I don't know, everyone's so much younger than me, I mean just two years, but it seems like...so it's lonely. But I'm taking this class on global health that I think is really...I met with the professor a couple times and I might help her with some research next summer in Mumbai, if the money works out.

LEO. Man, you work fast.

BEC. I walked into her office and I was like, I've built houses in Ecuador and taught English in Mali and installed solar panels in Kathmandu and I want to know how I can work with you.

And she was like, "Wow, it's so refreshing to meet a female undergraduate who doesn't end every sentence in a question mark."

So...

LEO. You always wanted to go to India.

BEC. It'll be so nice to travel somewhere not on my parents' dime, you know?

LEO. I could come.

BEC. ...to Mumbai?

LEO. Why not?

(Pause. The next two lines are simultaneous.)

BEC. / I want to break up.

LEO. I'm so happy to see you.
Whoa. Oh. Okay.

(pause)

Okay.

(He grins at her.)

BEC. The other night when I said I needed some time to think, that wasn't true, I want to break up. Sorry, I know the timing is shitty. I was gonna do it no matter what when you finished the bike trip, it's not...it's not about you going AWOL this summer, even though I'm really fucking pissed about that.

LEO. So you – huh. You were planning this for a while.

BEC. Yeah. Yes.

LEO. That's why you backed out of the bike trip.

BEC. Ummmmm....no, I backed out of the bike trip because I – I didn't *back out* of the bike trip, I was never definitely coming on the bike trip.

LEO. Uh, okay, I remember it differently but it really doesn't matter now, so.

BEC. You knew I was applying for internships, you knew that.

LEO. Yeah, and I knew you were buying gear and training and, like, telling me you loved me and it was important we got to spend this time together before you left for school. That's all.

BEC. Well, when Allison backed out –

LEO. Allison tore her ACL, dude, that's / totally –

BEC. Fine, but it wasn't gonna be the trip we'd planned, it wasn't gonna be the four of us.

LEO. But you admit that we had *planned* a trip, you *planned* to come with us, that was the *plan*. But I guess you were already planning to break up with me, you just didn't let me in on that.

BEC. I'm sorry I didn't come on the bike trip, okay?

LEO. No, it was good, it was amazing, actually, to have that time with Micah, so. I wouldn't trade that for anything.

BEC. Well good.

(brief pause)

LEO. I mean, it would have been nice to have you there when he was killed, it would have been nice to not be alone for that.

BEC. Yeah, it would have been nice if you'd showed up at the funeral, I really needed you then. Do you know how hurtful that was, and humiliating, that everyone was like, "Where the fuck is Leo?" and I was like "I don't know, he hasn't even *called me.*"

LEO. But you were already planning to break up with me.

(off her look)

What? I'm just, I'm trying to master this time line, Bec, it's a little confusing.

BEC. You're laying this all on me, but we had problems. We never had the kind of relationship Micah and Allison had, I think we should just face that.

LEO. We – ? I don't even know what that means.

BEC. They were like actual grown-ups in love, like really in love.

I'm not saying we didn't love each other –

LEO. No, you're saying I'm not a grown up.

BEC. I'm saying – even my mom still talks about it, what a mature, and, like, evenly-balanced-

LEO. Oh, well, if *Ellen* / thought so –

BEC. Don't be an asshole, you know what I mean, they just had this serenity that we –

LEO. I actually thought it was the other way around, that we were the ones with the real deal because I thought about you basically all the time when you weren't there and talked about you like some kind of pathetic lovesick idiot whereas Micah never thought about Ally at all.

BEC. That's because he didn't have to.

(brief pause)

LEO. I think you have some very weird very idealized picture of their relationship, because it might interest you to know that he cheated on her, actually.

BEC. Okay.

LEO. Like several times. With some extremely questionable specimens.

BEC. It's not cheating when it's an open relationship and it's really none of my business and I don't think it's cool at all to talk about him that way.

LEO. I just think it's interesting that your idea of a perfect relationship involves your boyfriend getting a BJ from the fifteen-year-old girl whose uncle owns the campground.

BEC. My idea of the perfect relationship involves feeling like I don't have to justify myself all the fucking time to someone who claims that they love me but is constantly disappointed in me. I am so tired of disappointing you, Leo.

And fuck you for telling me that about Micah, I did not want to know that.

*(**VERA** has entered with a laundry cart.)*

VERA. Excuse me.

I was going to the basement to do some laundry, I wondered if you have anything that needs to be washed.

LEO. No.

VERA. Are you sure? I haven't washed your sheets since you've / been here.

LEO. No!

Thanks.

(VERA exits slowly, with dignity.)

BEC. You know Micah's parents are back together, right?

LEO. …*what?*

BEC. I know.

LEO. Oh, no.

BEC. I actually tried to talk to them about it, I was like, "You know I love you both, but is this really a good idea? For you guys, and for Ethan?" It was so weird, I felt like such an adult.

LEO. What did they say?

BEC. He cried, and told me how proud he is of me, and how lucky Micah was to have me in his life, and she got super huffy and passive–aggressive and they both assured me that it's what Micah would have wanted. Which seems to me both patently false and completely irrelevant.

LEO. They're gonna destroy that poor kid.

BEC. And he's such a / sweet kid.

LEO. He's a good kid. He / really is.

BEC. It's a shit show, I give up.

(pause)

I gotta get back uptown.

LEO. Hold on, I want to read you something.

BEC. Leo, I'm already late.

LEO. It's short.

(He exits, then returns with a book of Rumi poetry. He takes a few moments to find the page.)

"There is a field."

That's the title.

BEC. Leo –

LEO. You have to promise to listen with an open heart.

BEC. I –

LEO. Please.

(She breathes, tries impatiently but earnestly to listen with an open heart.)

Out beyond ideas of wrongdoing
and rightdoing there is a field.

(He swallows. This is hard for him.)

I'll meet you there.
When the soul lies down in that grass
The world is too full to talk about.

(Pause. She sees he is almost overcome, puts a hand on him. He takes the opportunity to grab her and kiss her. She pushes him away.)

BEC. I have to go.

LEO. Let me touch you.

BEC. No.

LEO. You're forgetting how our bodies are together.

BEC. No, I'm not.

(She gently disentangles and moves away.)

When I'm not furious at you I'm really worried about you. I don't want you to become someone who makes me sad every time I think about you.

LEO. Okay, Bec, I'll go to *college*.

BEC. Fuck you.

LEO. One of us has turned our back on everything the four of us used to believe and it isn't me.

*(**VERA** reenters from the hall, without the cart but carrying detergent. **BEC** gathers her stuff angrily, tearfully, while **LEO** looks at the ground.)*

Hey.

*(**LEO** extends the pumpkin toward **BEC**, smiling idiotically. **BEC** ignores him and walks past **VERA** out the door without speaking. A silence.)*

VERA. Well.

Are you all right?

LEO. Yeah, I'm good.

VERA. She's lost weight.

(pause)

She could lose / some more –

LEO. *(quietly)* Shut up.

VERA. What?

LEO. *(with his grin, loudly)* It makes me sick to hear you talk about her body so just fucking stop, okay? Did you hear that?

(She is stunned. He exits into the bedroom.)

Scene Five

(*Several days later, around dusk.* **LEO** *and* **VERA** *sit, staring out into space. Something is different, though we don't know right away what it is. A silence.*)

VERA. Weren't you on a sailboat for a while?

LEO. Yeah. Yeah. In Mexico.

(*pause*)

VERA. And he was there? What's-his-name.

(*pause*)

Micah.

LEO. Yeah. He was there.

(*pause*)

And Ally was there too, for a while, but she got hepatitis and had to be evac-ed back to St. Paul.

VERA. Hepatitis? What were you eating?

LEO. Fish, mostly. Rice.

VERA. You caught the fish?

LEO. Yeah, with a, like. Harpoon kinda thing. You shoot them with this spear thing.

VERA. Aren't they fast?

LEO. Yeah.

VERA. Isn't it hard to hit them?

LEO. Yeah. They're fast. Micah was good at it.

(*pause*)

And the spear has a flotation device so after they're speared they rise to the surface.

(*pause*)

VERA. What does?

LEO. What?

VERA. I forget what we were talking about.

(*Pause. Pause.*)

LEO. Me too.

(more staring)

VERA. You know your father never did anything for me in bed.

(pause)

LEO. *What?* My father?

VERA. Yeah. Joe.

LEO. Joe was my grandfather.

VERA. Oh. Right.

*(**LEO** giggles.)*

Well he never did anything for me in bed. Neither of my husbands did. There was only one man who ever did anything for me in bed and it wasn't one of the ones I married.

LEO. Who was it?

VERA. My lips are sealed.

LEO. I won't tell.

VERA. Nope. Taking it with me to the grave.

(pause)

LEO. I've been incredibly horny since Micah died.

(pause)

VERA. Sure.

(pause)

LEO. Bec has kind of a weird pussy. But I like it.
Did you hear me?

VERA. Yes, but I don't want to discuss it.

(pause)

*(**LEO** picks up a bowl and lighter that we haven't noticed from the table.)*

LEO. You want some more?

VERA. No thank you, I didn't like the way it made my throat… Whaddayacallit.

(He lights and pulls.)

And I don't think it's really doing anything for me, besides.

LEO. *(holding the smoke in his lungs)* Were my parents ever in love?

(He exhales.)

VERA. Which ones are your parents? Oh right.

(She thinks.)

I never really understood your father. He's not very. Whaddayacallit.

(She thinks.)

Forthcoming. He doesn't…

LEO. Come forth?

(They both laugh.)

VERA. You know, your mother was always nervous. About… stupid things. She always thought she had offended someone, and then when she thinks that she starts acting peculiar and she does offend people.
What was the question?

LEO. Were my parents ever in love?

VERA. I think at first he made her stop worrying, and now he makes her worry more. But that's just what I think, and that and a dollar fifty will get me on the subway.

(pause)

LEO. Biggest regret?

VERA. Maybe I would have liked to have one of my own children. I didn't know I wanted one until I married Joe and his kids were around and then I thought, that would have been nice, to have one from the very beginning instead of coming in late like that.

(pause)

LEO. Thank you for celebrating the autumnal equinox with me this way.

(She nods.)

Scene Six

(In blackness, the sound of a key in the lock. Sound of a young woman giggling.)

(The door opens and light spills into the apartment from the hall. The giggling gets louder. **LEO** *enters with a drunk* **AMANDA** *leaning on him. He turns on a light.* **AMANDA** *is young-looking for nineteen – a pretty and fashion-forward Chinese-American woman. She alternately giggles and says, "shhhhhh!")*

LEO. It's okay, she's deaf.

AMANDA. Really? That's so sad!

LEO. You want a drink?

AMANDA. Yeah, what do you have?

LEO. *(with the liquor cabinet)* Uh…Campari?

AMANDA. This view is amaaaaaaaazing!

LEO. Uh, something that the label is too old to read…

AMANDA. I can't believe you live here. Do you just wake up every morning and think I can't believe I live here?

LEO. Not really.

AMANDA. What does she pay?

LEO. I dunno, I think she said like around twelve hundred.

(AMANDA screams.)

Shhhhh!

AMANDA. *(whispering)* Are you *serious*? Do you know how much my apartment costs?

LEO. I don't.

AMANDA. Eighteen hundred! It's about the size of this room! How long has she been here?

LEO. I don't know.

AMANDA. *(back with the view)* This is south, right?

LEO. Uh….

AMANDA. Did she watch the towers fall?

LEO. I have no idea.

AMANDA. You don't ask her nearly enough questions. If she was my grandma I'd know everything. I'm like obsessed with family history. If you want to know the names of all my great-grandmother's siblings in Chural Rina I'll…

(She cracks up.)

Rural. China. I'm drunk. Are you drunk?

(LEO pours two Camparis.)

LEO. I wasn't drinking.

AMANDA. You *weren't*? Are you gonna like date rape me?

LEO. *(nervous)* Uh…

AMANDA. I'm just kidding, I'll totally sleep with you. I mean probably. I like you. You're like a mountain man. Like a real live mountain man. Of the mountains. You live outside of society's, like…

(She can't think of how to finish the sentence. He hands her a Campari.)

LEO. I don't really know what this is, but it matches your bandaid.

AMANDA. Oh, yeah!

(She lifts a pinky finger, revealing a bright pink/orange bandaid.)

Did I tell you how I got this?

LEO. No.

AMANDA. I totally shut my finger in a cab door! If I showed you, you wouldn't believe it, it's like nine colors. I might not have a pinky fingernail ever again!

LEO. That's good, it's like your signature. Like your original thing.

AMANDA. But I'm already like a total freak, I mean look at me.

LEO. I don't think you're a freak.

AMANDA. *(disappointed)* You don't?

LEO. *(backtracking)* I mean –

AMANDA. I'm just teasing you, I'm just kidding. You're adorable, you're so cute.

LEO. I wanna see under it.

AMANDA. Under what? My bandaid?

LEO. Yeah, I wanna see the colors.

AMANDA. Ew! Gross! No! I mean, not *yet*.

(*She drinks some of the Campari.*)

Wow, this is nasty.

LEO. Sorry, I can –

AMANDA. No, in a good way.

(*A flirtatious pause. He leans in for the kiss. She ducks coquettishly away and goes back to the window.*)

So what's your deal, mountain man?

LEO. My – ?

AMANDA. I'll tell you my deal first, that's only fair. I'm at Parsons, duh. I sort of have a boyfriend but mostly not right now. I grew up in San Francisco, my parents run like a dim sum empire, so I'm kinda rich and I don't really like to apologize for it. Um, my sister is five years older and she already has two kids which I think is so gross. Like I can't even stand to be in her house because of the smell. And I'm gonna be an international art star, that much is clear, though I don't know exactly what medium yet.

Your turn.

LEO. Um, I'm from St. Paul. And…now I'm here, by way of Seattle.

(*brief pause*)

AMANDA. Wow, you're really, like, milking this man of few words, romantic scruffy beard thing.

LEO. I just really want to kiss you, Amelia.

AMANDA. Am / anda.

LEO. Amanda! Sorry! I knew I was gonna do that.

AMANDA. Yeah, that just set you back, like, at least twenty minutes.

LEO. Amanda Amanda Amanda Amanda Amanda.

AMANDA. You should do that inside your head instead of out loud.

LEO. Sorry.

AMANDA. Your name is Leo, which means Lion. What's your astrological sign?

LEO. Not Leo. Virgo.

AMANDA. Mine's Libra.

(She mimes scales.)

Balance.

LEO. You're really beautiful, Amanda.

AMANDA. That's good, keep practicing my name, soon you won't even have to think about it.

LEO. I'm sorry, I'm really not an asshole.

AMANDA. Who's Amelia. Ex-girlfriend?

LEO. No, I – don't take this the wrong way, but I think I did that because all night I was afraid I was gonna call you Lily? Which is my sister's name? You sorta remind me of her.

AMANDA. *(a joke)* Is she Chinese?

LEO. Yeah.

AMANDA. Seriously?

LEO. Yeah, she's adopted.

AMANDA. And she's an amazing dresser? No, that's a joke. But seriously, is she?

LEO. No, she's much more, like…Banana Republic than you.

AMANDA. Ooh.

LEO. But it's just, something in the…

(He gestures vaguely toward his face.)

I dunno.

AMANDA. That's sweet, mountain man. I think that's really sweet.

Where is she?

LEO. St. Paul. With my parents. She was in college, but then she took a semester off, and now it's like her third year off, and she's not really sure what she's doing. I'm kinda worried about her.

AMANDA. What's she good at?

LEO. She has the most amazing voice in the world. She sounds like a songbird, I know that's a fucking cliché, but if you were in the woods and you heard her singing, you would seriously think it was like the most talented bird you had ever heard.

AMANDA. You miss her.

LEO. Yeah.

AMANDA. Why are you here?

LEO. Well, my grandma's really old, and she doesn't really have anybody, so. I thought it would be cool to come spend some time with her.

AMANDA. That is *so sweet!*

LEO. I don't really see it that way, as, like, a favor? She's just like a really good friend who I happen to be related to.

AMANDA. You might be too good to be true, new friend. You might be.

(*He moves slowly toward her. She dodges him and goes to the bookshelf.*)

I don't know why I'm feeling kind of shy, it's uncharacteristic, I'm usually pretty slutty.

(*with a book*)

Is your grandmother like a communist?

LEO. Card carrying.

AMANDA. (*alarmed*) Seriously?!

LEO. Yeah. Why?

AMANDA. Oh my God. Oh my God. I'm sorry. I like, *hate* Communists.

LEO. What? Why?

AMANDA. Duh! I'm Chinese! Why do you think my family left?

LEO. Oh.

AMANDA. Why do you think your *sister* was put up for *adoption?* Because the communists like fucked China up the ass!

LEO. Um, I'm not sure if / that's –

AMANDA. Oh it is. That is *literally* what happened.

LEO. Okay…sorry?

AMANDA. Are *you* a communist?

LEO. Um…no.

AMANDA. You had to think about that.

(He tries to kiss her again.)

Dude! I'm not sure I can get it on in a communist's apartment, I'm really not.

LEO. A lot of people were communists back then – it was like, it was like…recycling, or whatever.

AMANDA. What?

LEO. Like it was cool, it was something you did to be, you know, responsible. To society. I'm not a communist, I swear, I'm not.

AMANDA. *(seriously)* My family didn't do so well over there, okay? I know I'm like this funny weird girl in platform shoes, but I actually am not joking at all and would get really upset if I told you what happened.

(long pause)

LEO. My best friend died this summer.

(She looks at him.)

We were biking across the country together and he died. That's why I'm here. Because I don't know where else to be.
Amanda.

(A long pause. She grabs his face. They kiss passionately. **VERA** *enters, disoriented. She doesn't have her teeth in so her lips curl over her gums. They don't hear her and continue, with hands moving all over each other. She sees what's going on, startles slightly, and then realizes*

what she's looking at. She turns to go, but **AMANDA,** *in a moment of pulling away and opening her eyes, sees her and screams. They separate.)*

AMANDA. Oh my God!

VERA. *(holding up a hand)* Excuse me.

(She exits.)

AMANDA. Oh my *God!* That scared the *shit* out of me! She looked like a ghost! She looked like a little white haired old lady ghost!

LEO. Here, come to my room.

AMANDA. Hold on, that really freaked me out!

LEO. Okay, okay.

(She goes to sit on the couch. He tentatively sits near her and rubs her back.)

It's cool. She doesn't care.

AMANDA. I don't want to get old and lose all my teeth, that shit is so *fucked.*

LEO. Shhhhhhh.

(He continues to rub her back. She begins to relax. He moves in a little closer.)

AMANDA. What was your friend's name?

(brief pause)

LEO. Micah.

AMANDA. How did he die?

(He stops rubbing her back.)

Sorry.

LEO. No, you're right, the old lady kinda killed the mood.

(long pause)

AMANDA. God, is tomorrow Tuesday?

LEO. I'm not sure.

AMANDA. I actually have class really early, I totally forgot that. I know it sounds like a lame excuse, but it's actually true.

LEO. It's fine.

AMANDA. Are you gonna have blue balls or anything?

LEO. No.

AMANDA. I feel kinda bad.

LEO. Don't.

AMANDA. I could give you my number…?

(He doesn't respond.)

Ohhhhh*kay.*

LEO. I just, I probably wouldn't use it? So…

(She stands. She's not sure what to do, so she just walks to the door. She has trouble with the lock. He goes to the door and unlocks it. She turns to him, angry, ashamed.)

AMANDA. I'm glad I didn't let you see under my bandaid.

(She exits.)

Scene Seven

(The middle of the night. **LEO** *is sitting in darkness.)*

*(***VERA*** *enters in her nightgown and turns on a light. Seeing* **LEO**, *she turns it off. It's actually dark as opposed to "stage dark" so that we can only see their silhouettes against the window. She goes and sits near him. A silence.)*

LEO. So we were in Kansas, because – even though that was way out of the way we wanted to hit the center of the country, preferably around the fourth of July for maximum earnestness slash unacknowledged irony factor. The timing worked out so it was July 3rd and we were approaching Gypsum, our small town America of choice, one bar, one diner, seventeen churches or whatever. And we were going west to east, so, wind at our backs. The wind comes out of the south in the summer, but more like the southwest, so in a way going west to east was a pussy move on our parts, but we kind of wanted to do the opposite of the historical – like American is east to west, so we were going the opposite way, also we lived out west, so. It was more honest to start there.

Western Kansas is like ass flat, the cliché, so you're basically just riding the wind and if you pedal even a little bit in a low gear you hit fifteen mph no problem. Fifteen mph is a slow speed in a car, but on a bike it's pretty good, it's pretty good. So it's morning and the sun's pretty low; between the low sun and the flat ride and the good wind it's the perfect time to take shadow pictures. That means you take a picture of your own shadow while you're riding, totally a staple of the cross country bike trip, gotta have the shadow picture, and with our huge packs and panniers we were gonna have especially dope shadow pictures. Micah thinks he's a really good photographer, he thinks he has talent, so he's doing a lot of bullshit with shutter speed and framing and what have you and we're both taking shadow

LEO. *(cont.)* pictures and we hear a truck coming behind us, or I hear it, I assume Micah does, I think he does because we both hug the shoulder a little bit, still taking our shadow shots, and the truck gets louder and closer and passes us and I see it's a Tyson truck full of fucking crates of screaming chickens packed together and there are feathers flying out of the truck bed like some kind of I don't know what kind of metaphor, and I scream up to Micah who did I mention was in front of me, "Look at that fucking slave poultry!" And he looks back at me, he has his left hand on his handlebar and his right hand still on his bullshit professional camera and he looks back at me and he's laughing and he starts to say something but the truck bed separates from the cab and flies backward and takes him off the road.

(silence, save for city sounds)

Before the ambulance came this PR lady from Tyson came. I didn't realize I was still holding my camera. She was like, "I'm sorry sir, but I have to confiscate your camera." She has to yell it for me to hear her over all these maimed and freaked out birds. I was like, "My best friend is under three thousand chickens." She was like, "I understand you're upset, but this will be easier for both of us if you just give me your camera now." I was like, "I couldn't get to him, he's buried under there, where is the fucking ambulance?" And she was like, "I'm going to ask you one more time – " and I threw my camera on the ground.

(silence)

So what I don't have is these pictures from Wyoming, we did these stupid corny timer shots at the top of the Continental Divide, in front of the sign that says the altitude and all that shit, there was still snow up there in June. He caught a fish in Yellowstone, with his bare hands, he stood really still and reached in and…I had a picture of him holding up this fish longer than his head and neck. Oh and we dipped our back tires in the Pacific, that's another corny thing you do, because then you're supposed to dip your front tires in the Atlantic when you get there. Which I have not done yet, incidentally, don't know why. And I got a little video of him dipping his back tire and pretending to fall off this rock into the sea because he was a fucking clown, you know, he was a gifted physical comedian, he could have done that for real.

And then there are all the pictures of him I don't remember taking, and maybe losing those is worse than losing the ones I do.

(silence)

It took them about forty five minutes to get him out, and the funny thing was he hadn't sustained any trauma to his head or anything but he had been face down in the mud with hundreds of pounds of weight on him and he had suffocated.

(silence)

So the part that everyone's pissed at me about is that after I filled out all the paperwork at the police station and called his mom and my mom I got back on my bike and kept riding.

(long silence)

VERA. I'm not wearing my hearing aid. So I could only hear parts of what you said. But I didn't want to interrupt.

(He lies down on the couch with his head in **VERA***'s lap.)*

Scene Eight

*(**VERA** is on the phone, sitting with pen and paper in hand.)*

VERA. Are you sure that's it?

I don't think that sounds right.

I said I don't think that sounds right.

*(A long pause, in which **VERA** becomes gradually more taken aback.)*

Is that what I said? I didn't say I don't appreciate your looking it up for me, I do appreciate that. I just said I don't think that sounds right. And it's a cause I've been giving to for a long time, so I would think I would recognize the address.

(brief pause)

Well it doesn't! If it doesn't sound right, I'm not supposed to say so? Just to be polite?

(brief pause)

How should I know? Maybe you picked up the wrong piece of paper, or it's from an old, whaddayacallit.

No, I don't know what it is, if I did I wouldn't have called you, now that's really a stupid question.

(Moves the phone away from her ear, and perhaps we can hear Ginny yelling, though we can't distinguish what she's saying.)

Oh for crying out loud, just tell it to me again, I'll say that's wonderful, that sounds exactly right, and I really owe you, Ginny, for taking two minutes out of your busy life to give me the wrong goddamn address.

(She is poised to write.)

Hello?

Ginny?

*(Furious, **VERA** goes to the phone and hangs up. She thinks about it for a moment, then picks up and dials*

*Ginny's number – it's a rotary phone, remember, so it
takes a long time. She waits. Maybe we can hear Ginny's
phone ringing distantly across the hall, and her answer-
ing machine picking up.* **VERA** *speaks with utter, cool
clarity.)*

VERA. *(cont.)* Hello, Ginny, I know you're there and you're
not picking up because you're like a child. Anyway, I
wanted to let you know that there's no need to call
me from now on because with my grandson here I'm
really very well taken care of and I don't need anyone
else checking in. And since it's obviously so difficult
for you to be in touch with me I think that's best.

*(She hangs up. She is immediately remorseful. She brings
her hand to her mouth.* **LEO** *enters. He touches her head
on his way into the kitchen.* **VERA** *picks up the phone
again, thinks, then hangs up.* **LEO** *reenters with orange
juice.)*

LEO. Ginny?

(She nods absently, and puts her hearing aid back in.)

Don't you ever just go over there and knock on the
door? You know she's like twenty feet away.

VERA. For some reason we've never done that. Some idea
she has about privacy, or…

(She trails off.)

LEO. You okay?

VERA. My files are such a mess. It's the time of the year I
usually do all my donations and I can't find the list of
charities I give to and I can't find my checkbook, so.
That's the kind of morning I'm having.

LEO. I can help you look if you still haven't found it when
I get back.

VERA. Where are you going?

LEO. Climbing wall, garden, interview.

VERA. Interview? For what?

LEO. For a job.

(brief pause)

VERA. Well I think that's pretty terrific. You're thinking about getting a part time job, is that it?

LEO. Full time. Very full time.

VERA. I never thought I'd see the day!

LEO. Hey, I have no aversion to work, it's just gotta be the right job.

VERA. Where is it?

LEO. Rockies.

VERA. What?

LEO. Rocky Mountains.

VERA. *(hiding her disappointment)* Oh.

LEO. They're looking for counselors, they have this program where they drop a bunch of rich kids in the mountains, they have to get from one point to another, rich kids have no idea what the fuck's what, they need leaders, so.

It's actually a pretty cool program, I did it in high school. Gotta say I think I'm very qualified, I think I have a good shot.

VERA. So when would that start?

LEO. Not till next summer.

VERA. *(relieved)* Oh.

LEO. But I'd go out early, spend the winter on the slopes, there's always work for people like me.

VERA. So when would you leave?

LEO. I don't know. Soon.

VERA. I see.

(pause)

You know, you really haven't given the city a chance, you haven't done any of the museums, or the theater –

LEO. Grandma, come on.

VERA. I'm not trying to convince you of anything, I'm just making an observation. It's a great place to live and you haven't had the experience of it, not really.

LEO. I'm like a caged bird here, Vera, it's nothing against your city, but for me it's like a concrete prison.

VERA. Oh that's just a lot of – whaddayacallit – new-age baloney and you should listen to yourself once in a while because you sound stupid, you really do.

(A silence. LEO *exits into his bedroom. After a moment, he reenters with his backpack.)*

LEO. So I'll be back in a few hours, and then if you still need help looking for your, uh...

VERA. You didn't take it, did you?

LEO. What?

VERA. My checkbook.

Listen, I'll be a lot less angry if you tell me now.

LEO. *(smiling)* I didn't take it.

(pause)

VERA. Leo Joseph-Connell–

LEO. I didn't take it! I didn't take it I didn't take it I didn't take it. Yesterday you lost your keys, there were three days you couldn't find your hearing aid, there was the priceless morning your teeth went missing, you think I took those too? I didn't take your fucking checkbook. God.

(pause)

VERA. I hope you're telling the truth, I really do. Your records of how much money you've taken haven't exactly been...I wasn't going to say anything, but...

(pause)

LEO. Well let's hope this interview goes well, because it's clear you don't trust me and it would be better for both of us if I got out of here.

VERA. Maybe that's true.

LEO. Maybe.

VERA. If you're going to the garden before the – you should bring a change of clothes because you always get filthy there.

LEO. I thought of that.

VERA. You did.

Well.

(She gazes off absently. He exits. The noise of the door closing startles her.)

Scene Nine

(LEO on Skype. It's late in the afternoon. He sits in front of an open laptop in a corner of the apartment.)

LEO. Can you hear me? Lily?

Can you – oh, hey.

(He waves once, slowly, smiling.)

I can see that big smile but I can't hear you. Oh, hold up –

(He hits the volume key several times. We hear LILY's voice very faintly through the monitor.)

LILY. *(offstage)* …can just call me –

LEO. Hey! There / it is –

LILY. *(offstage)* Hey!

LEO. Hey, sis, yeah.

(A pause. He smiles genuinely. Lily laughs through the monitor.)

LILY. *(offstage)* Where's Grandma?

LEO. She's out shopping.

LILY. *(offstage)* What kind of computer does she have?

LEO. It's a…

(He looks.)

It's a MacBook, it's pretty new, actually. She still had that plastic covering on the screen.

(laughter from LILY through the computer)

She's so scared of it, she probably thought if she took it off the whole thing would fall apart.

(more laughter)

I've been trying to get her to use it so she'll have more…because I've been here three weeks now and I know there are some days if I wasn't here she wouldn't see anyone. What am I talking about how are you how are you how / are you.

LILY. *(offstage)* – I'm okay –

LEO. I'm sorry I haven't been in touch –

LILY. *(offstage)* Yeah, Mom's really –

LEO. Can we not talk about Mom?

LILY. *(offstage)* …okay.

(A silence. He lifts the computer and angles it around the room, allowing her to see the apartment.)

LEO. You remember this place?

LILY. *(offstage)* …yeah.

(brief pause)

LEO. You remember singing at Grandpa's memorial service?

LILY. *(offstage)* …vaguely.

LEO. Aunt Beth brought that shitty Casio and accompanied you, badly.

*(**LILY** laughs.)*

You sang "The Water is Wide." In English *and* in French.

LILY. *(offstage)* I can't believe / you remember that.

LEO. I was proud of you. You brought some talented fucking genetic code with you into this family.

*(A pause. Maybe we can hear **LILY** sigh.)*

I was thinking you should maybe come out here for a while. Stay with Grandma. They gotta have like the / best voice teachers in the world here –

LILY. *(offstage)* Wait, you're cutting out.

/ Leo, I can't hear you.

Can you hear me?

LEO. Can you hear me?

Lil, can you still not hear me?

Yeah, I can hear you.

LILY. *(offstage)* Oh there you are.

LEO. You can hear me again?

LILY. *(offstage)* Now I can, yeah.

LEO. Sorry, I'm jacking a neighbor's wifi, I'm only getting like / one bar.

LILY. *(offstage)* It's okay.

(Pause. He smiles at her, presumably getting a big, sad smile back.)

LEO. So I, hey, I wanted to ask, um, are you...? In therapy? I mean it's cool, obviously it's cool if you are.

I just. I wondered if, uh, and this is probably really stupid? If, and obviously it's not just one thing, but if, like, it had to do with...

When I was home, earlier this summer, and we had that party, and we were fucked up...?

LILY. *(offstage)* Um...I...I don't know / if I...

LEO. No, yeah, I get that. I mean, I guess that's why you go to therapy, right, so you *don't* have to talk about these things with your immediate...

But if it was that – thing, (let me just say this,) I would like to apologize, and say I one hundred per cent feel like a dick if that was weird or awkward or made you feel less like my *actual* sister, which obviously you are. Because I think you're like the greatest sister known to human history and I would like to not have fucked at least that one thing up, okay? Lil?

LILY. *(offstage)* ...please come home...

LEO. Yeah, I just...I have to give some thought to whether that would be the best thing for everyone. And I don't just mean me, I mean Mom, and you, and...everyone.

But I'll think about it. It would be good to see you.

Yeah, I'm gonna hang up now, sorry.

(He closes the laptop. He takes a breath and regains control. The phone rings. Sure it is Lily calling back, he shakes it out, grins, and picks up.)

Yeah, hey, sorry bout that.

Hello?

(He listens.)

Hello? Who is this?

LEO. *(cont.)* I'm sorry, I...I can't understand what you're saying.

(Pause. Discomfited, he hangs up. He gets the laptop and begins to head toward **VERA***'s room to put it back. He is stopped by the sound of a sickening thud [and maybe something breaking?] in the direction of Ginny's apartment. He stands still, listening. It's silent. He continues to* **VERA***'s room with the laptop. After a moment, he returns without the laptop. He sits on the couch, uneasy.)*

(A long while passes. He listens, but there is no more sound. He makes a decision, stands, and goes to Ginny's door. He knocks.)

Scene Ten

(Mid-afternoon, a few days later.)

*(**LEO** is wearing a suit that is too big and from an era long past – Joe's.)*

*(**VERA** enters from her bedroom, also dressed up.)*

VERA. Five minutes?

LEO. Whenever you're ready.

VERA. I just have to make peepee.

*(She is about to exit, but sees something. She comes over to **LEO** to fix his tie. He lets her.)*

I found my checkbook. You don't need to say anything, I was wrong about that, and I'm sorry.

LEO. I do owe you some money. I didn't write it down where you said but I know how much it is. I'll pay you back.

VERA. Maybe you will, maybe you won't. But I appreciate your saying so.

(She finishes his tie.)

I wish I could say you look just like him, but you really don't. You look more like your father's side of the family.

LEO. Sorry.

VERA. But you look good.

(She does a Brooklyn-y accent.)

You clean up real nice!

LEO. I feel like a clown.

VERA. You look a little bit like a clown, but you look good.

(She is about to exit.)

LEO. Grandma.

VERA. Hm?

LEO. You can see your bra, through that shirt.

VERA. I know. This is the bra I wear with this shirt, because it goes.

(She exits into the bathroom. The buzzer sounds. He looks off, then decides to answer himself.)

LEO. Hello?

BEC. *(through the intercom)* It's Bec.

(After a moment of uncertainty, he buzzes her in. He looks at himself, sorta freaks out, takes off his jacket, starts to unbutton his pants.)

LEO. Fuck it.

(He puts his jacket back on. He tousles his own hair. He tries to look casual. A knock at the door.)

It's open.

*(**BEC** enters. She is wearing bike shorts and a long-sleeved jersey. She is carrying her helmet.)*

BEC. Hey.

LEO. ...hey.

BEC. Nice suit.

LEO. Thanks. Nice jersey.

BEC. Thanks.

(pause)

LEO. Uh...

BEC. So this is really stupid, I should've called, I thought you might want to go on a bike ride, but you're obviously busy.

LEO. Yeah. Yeah, I am kind of busy.

BEC. Okay, so. Sorry. Never mind.

(She goes to leave.)

LEO. Uh. I would say we could go tomorrow, but I'm heading out.

BEC. Where?

LEO. Back to St. Paul for a couple days, face up to the family. Then to Colorado.

BEC. What's in Colorado?

LEO. Got a job.

BEC. Congratulations.

LEO. Yeah, I think it's gonna be cool. Clarifying. Mountain air and all that.

BEC. That's great, I'm really happy for you.

LEO. Thanks. Yeah.

If you could wait maybe a couple hours – ?

BEC. I have class.

LEO. Right. Class.

(*pause*)

BEC. It's just, I thought maybe you'd want to dip your front tire.

LEO. Ah.

BEC. Because you asked me to go with you that night you showed up at my apartment, and I was not in a frame of mind to…but you've probably already done it by now.

LEO. No, it's been kinda crazy around here, my grandma's needed me a lot. Her neighbor died. That's where we're –

BEC. I'm so sorry.

LEO. Not your fault.

BEC. I know.

Well. You probably won't have time, but, I printed a couple maps. Depending on where you want to do it. I know open ocean is ideal but around here I think you're gonna have to settle for bay.

LEO. I think as long as it's salty it counts.

BEC. I'm actually, one of the classes I'm taking, it's an anthropology class about ritual? Like in societies all over the world, and how it, on like a psychological and even neurological basis, it…well we're not that far into the class yet, but basically every culture has them and that's because they work. I don't know, I think if you can fit it in, you should do it.

(*She hands him the maps.*)

LEO. Thanks.

(*The sound of a toilet flushing.* **VERA** *enters, putting pearls over her head. She sees* **BEC.***)*

VERA. Oh.

BEC. Hi.

VERA. Hello.

(**VERA** *looks to* **LEO,** *who doesn't explain.*)

LEO. You ready?

VERA. Just about.

LEO. I'm just gonna grab the notes for my speech.

(*He exits.* **VERA** *is thoroughly mystified.*)

VERA. You're coming, is that it?

BEC. No. I was just…no.

I'm sorry about your neighbor.

VERA. You know Leo was the one who brought her to the hospital. He took care of everything, he stayed with her until they brought her into the, whaddayacallit. He was really…he was very much a man. Oh I'm sorry, you don't like it when I put it that way.

BEC. No, I'm actually glad to hear it.

VERA. He's leaving tomorrow, I guess he told you. Which does not make me very happy.

BEC. I'm sorry.

VERA. You'd think at my age I'd know better than to get used to anything.

(*off* **BEC**'s *stricken look*)

Oh don't look at me like that, I'll be all right, I've always been all right.

BEC. I know, I wasn't…*pitying* you, or –

VERA. Well you were, but never mind.

BEC. I wasn't, please don't think that.

VERA. All right, I always manage to upset you, let's forget I said anything.

BEC. You didn't upset me, I mean it's not you, I'm just irretrievably sad right now, and I know it's gonna pass, I know that, but it's very *convincing*, while it lasts, you know? It just feels very very real.

VERA. Well, it is real. That's why. But you're right. It'll pass.

*(**LEO** reenters, unaware of what he is interrupting.)*

LEO. Okay!
What?

(pause)

BEC. Bye, Leo.

(brief pause)

LEO. Bye.

*(They hug deeply. **VERA** averts her eyes.)*

BEC. Bye Vera.

VERA. Take care of yourself.

*(**BEC** exits. A long pause.)*

VERA. What's this about a speech?

LEO. I wasn't sure if they were gonna open it up to people in the audience. But just in case.
You said she doesn't have a lot of people.

VERA. But did you ever meet her? I mean, before – ?

LEO. No. You're right, it's probably not a good idea.

VERA. I think it's a lovely idea, I'm just surprised. Do you want to practice? We have a few minutes.

LEO. Uh…

(He looks at the paper.)

Nah.

VERA. You should always practice before public speaking. Joe would've told you that.

LEO. Okay, um…
I feel weird. Um. *(He refers occasionally to his notes over the following.)* Ginny was my grandmother's across / the hall

VERA. Loudly, please.

(brief pause)

LEO. Ginny was my grandmother's across the hall neighbor, and they used to call each other every night to check in. Which I know gave my mom and my uncles a lot of solace, that there was someone my grandma talked to every day. But I don't want to make it sound like that was Ginny's only purpose in life, because actually a google search revealed a varied and fascinating past. Ginny was an actress a long time ago, and she understudied for a play on Broadway called "Mary Had a Little."

(to VERA)

You didn't tell me that.

(VERA nods.)

After that she started working for the William Morris Agency, as a secretary. So I guess she decided if she wasn't making it as an actor she wanted to help other actors make it, which I think is a pretty productive way of dealing with that kind of disappointment.

Also she was married to a man who was killed in the Korean War. And after that I think she didn't get married again...?

(He looks to VERA, who nods.)

So I don't know, but I bet that was really terrible, and I know she was a peace activist, like my grandma, so I guess she came at that from a pretty personal angle.

That's all I could find on the internet but she was eighty-one years old so there was a lot of other stuff, too.

(pause)

I guess that's not such a good ending.

VERA. It needs maybe one more.../ whaddayacallit.

LEO. Yeah.

(They think, for kind of a long time.)

VERA. It's hard, because the truth is she was a pain in the ass.

(pause)

I guess you could say...you could say something about all her plants.

LEO. Oh yeah, I saw, in her apartment, there was like a / forest.

VERA. She would get a, whaddayacallit, that green slimy thing from California, with a stone / in it –

LEO. An avocado?

VERA. She would get an avocado at the supermarket, and put the stone in some water with those, uh, toothpicks, and next thing you know it's a tree.

What is that expression?

(She thinks.)

Green thumb.

(She is relieved to have thought of this.)

She was a pain in the ass, but god, she was like a magician. That woman could make anything grow.

*(**LEO** listens, and then writes. Lights fade.)*

End of Play

SAMUEL FRENCH STAFF

Nate Collins
President

Ken Dingledine
Director of Operations,
Vice President

Bruce Lazarus
Executive Director,
General Counsel

Rita Maté
Director of Finance

ACCOUNTING

Lori Thimsen | Director of Licensing Compliance
Nehal Kumar | Senior Accounting Associate
Josephine Messina | Accounts Payable
Helena Mezzina | Royalty Administration
Joe Garner | Royalty Administration
Jessica Zheng | Accounts Receivable
Andy Lian | Accounts Receivable
Zoe Qiu | Accounts Receivable
Charlie Sou | Accounting Associate
Joann Mannello | Orders Administrator

BUSINESS AFFAIRS

Lysna Marzani | Director of Business Affairs
Kathryn McCumber | Business Administrator

CUSTOMER SERVICE AND LICENSING

Brad Lohrenz | Director of Licensing Development
Fred Schnitzer | Business Development Manager
Laura Lindson | Licensing Services Manager
Kim Rogers | Professional Licensing Associate
Matthew Akers | Amateur Licensing Associate
Ashley Byrne | Amateur Licensing Associate
Glenn Halcomb | Amateur Licensing Associate
Derek Hassler | Amateur Licensing Associate
Jennifer Carter | Amateur Licensing Associate
Kelly McCready | Amateur Licensing Associate
Annette Storckman | Amateur Licensing Associate
Chris Lonstrup | Outgoing Information Specialist

EDITORIAL AND PUBLICATIONS

Amy Rose Marsh | Literary Manager
Ben Coleman | Editorial Associate
Gene Sweeney | Graphic Designer
David Geer | Publications Supervisor
Charlyn Brea | Publications Associate
Tyler Mullen | Publications Associate

MARKETING

Abbie Van Nostrand | Director of Corporate
Communications
Ryan Pointer | Marketing Manager
Courtney Kochuba | Marketing Associate

OPERATIONS

Joe Ferreira | Product Development Manager
Casey McLain | Operations Supervisor
Danielle Heckman | Office Coordinator, Reception

SAMUEL FRENCH BOOKSHOP (LOS ANGELES)

Joyce Mehess | Bookstore Manager
Cory DeLair | Bookstore Buyer
Jennifer Palumbo | Customer Service Associate
Sonya Wallace | Bookstore Associate
Tim Coultas | Bookstore Associate
Monté Patterson | Bookstore Associate
Robin Hushbeck | Bookstore Associate
Alfred Contreras | Shipping & Receiving

LONDON OFFICE

Felicity Barks | Rights & Contracts Associate
Steve Blacker | Bookshop Associate
David Bray | Customer Services Associate
Zena Choi | Professional Licensing Associate
Robert Cooke | Assistant Buyer
Stephanie Dawson | Amateur Licensing Associate
Simon Ellison | Retail Sales Manager
Jason Felix | Royalty Administration
Susan Griffiths | Amateur Licensing Associate
Robert Hamilton | Amateur Licensing Associate
Lucy Hume | Publications Manager
Nasir Khan | Management Accountant
Simon Magniti | Royalty Administration
Louise Mappley | Amateur Licensing Associate
James Nicolau | Despatch Associate
Martin Phillips | Librarian
Zubayed Rahman | Despatch Associate
Steve Sanderson | Royalty Administration Supervisor
Douglas Schatz | Acting Executive Director
Roger Sheppard | I.T. Manager
Geoffrey Skinner | Company Accountant
Peter Smith | Amateur Licensing Associate
Garry Spratley | Customer Service Manager
David Webster | UK Operations Director